Louis Kinney Harlow

The World's Best Hymns

Louis Kinney Harlow

The World's Best Hymns

ISBN/EAN: 9783744779135

Printed in Europe, USA, Canada, Australia, Japan

Cover: Foto ©Andreas Hilbeck / pixelio.de

More available books at **www.hansebooks.com**

THE

WORLD'S BEST HYMNS

Compiled and Illustrated

By LOUIS K. HARLOW

WITH AN INTRODUCTION

By J. W. CHURCHILL

New Edition

WITH ADDITIONAL HYMNS

BOSTON

LITTLE, BROWN, AND COMPANY

1893

University Press:

John Wilson and Son, Cambridge.

INDEX OF FIRST LINES.

v

Index of First Lines.

Index of First Lines.

INDEX OF AUTHORS.

Index of Authors.

Index of Authors.

NOTE. — Hymns by Longfellow, Whittier, Holmes, and Mrs. Stowe are included by permission of Messrs. Houghton, Mifflin, and Company.

INTRODUCTION.

IT is a pleasant office to introduce to the thoughtful portion of the reading public the selections which the taste and enthusiasm of my friend, Mr. Louis K. Harlow, have prepared for its benefit and enjoyment. His congenial task has been guided by the simple, practical aim of bringing together in a convenient and an attractive form the choicest specimens of sacred poetry that have gradually grown up in the soil of religious sentiment. This compilation is not a hymn-book, but a book of hymns. Neither is it an abounding treasure-house of religious verse. Exquisite collections of sacred song have already been made for poetry's sake, with the avowed purpose of admitting no poetical composition, however good its intention, unless it has been

touched with the power and magic of high
poetic art. Still other religious poems have
been gathered, with the paramount aim of direct
usefulness in ministering to the nurture and solace of the spiritual life. This book enters into
no rivalry with such incomparable volumes of
religious poetry, each one a noble library in
itself. The present editor's aim and scope pur-
posely have been confined to certain special
limits.

The leading principle of choice which has
been followed is the selection of the best Eng-
lish lyrical religious poetry that has been im-
mediately associated with sacred music, and
hallowed by long and constant use in the service of song in the home and the church. They
are lyrics that have become classic as *hymns*,
rather than through their literary excellence of
poetic form. In the perusal of most of them
the mental ear will catch the undertone of the
sacred melodies to which they have usually
been sung.

Nor has the taste and discernment of the editor failed to detect the enhancing worth of poetical merit in the expression of thought and sentiment whose chief excellence lies in its spiritual value. A hymn as a mode of poetry has the object of all poetic art, — the spontaneous expression of emotion on the part of the writer, and the excitement of corresponding emotion in the heart of the reader or singer. It is at once the fervid, sincere transcript and impression of some phase of spiritual life cast in a metrical mould. The spiritual emotions of Penitence and Praise, of Faith, Hope, Love, and aspirations after Perfection, are all the more inspiring, penetrating, and influential, when embodied in choice, melodious diction and beautiful form.

A Christian hymn has its peculiar canons of excellence. It is either written or appropriated for popular use; it is chiefly employed as an integral part of public worship; the vast majority of those who sing it are plain people. Hence, our best hymns, while fervid in spirit, are simple in diction and chastened in imagery. With its confessedly practical aim of edifying the inner life, the ideal hymn is saved from the peril of didactics — the sure death of poetry — by lines so deftly wrought that they quickly catch the ear of the little child, and linger in the memory of the aged when almost every other form of language is forgotten. A hymn as a question of poetic art is a matter of execution. In structure and movement it has a beginning, a middle, and an end. "In a hymn," remarks that skilful hymn-writer, James Montgomery, "there should be a manifest gradation in the thoughts, and their mutual dependence should be so perceptible that they could not be transposed without injuring the unity of the piece; every line carrying forward the connection, and every stanza adding a well-proportioned limb to a symmetrical body. The reader should know when the strain is complete, and be satisfied as at the close of an air of music."

This high ideal of what a hymn should be seems more or less consciously to have been borne in mind in the choice of the selections before us; nearly every hymn successfully stands the test. Many of them are master-pieces of lyric poetry, which all English-speaking people have agreed in admiring. They have been written by acknowledged masters of song, and have secured a wide and enduring fame.

The restricted rule of choice which influenced the compiler in his selection has, no doubt, been modified in some instances by his personal preferences. He may be assured that those hymns which have charmed and moved an intelligent lover of sacred poetry will probably delight others. And yet these selections are remarkably free from mere individual predilection. They are representative and catholic. They are not chosen for any one class of Christians, but for our common Christian life. The balance of personal judgment has been kept most true; it would be difficult to infer a system of religious opinions from the poems presented.

Obviously, no two persons would make precisely the same selection from such a wide range of choice in the almost limitless field of religious poetry. Many readers will doubtless expect to find some familiar hymn, and feel disappointed at its absence. The omission can sometimes be accounted for by the exercise of the editor's critical judgment. The " Fountain filled with blood, drawn from Emmanuel's veins," is a favorite hymn, found in nearly every hymn-book in the churches. Surprise will perhaps be expressed by some at the omission of Cowper's famous hymn from this collection. Others will commend its exclusion because of its imagery, although to the gentle poet of Olney it was a vivid and reverent description of the chief article of his faith. Let it be noted, however, that other hymns are found here that acknowledge and interpret the same great Christian fact. Other omissions can very likely be attributed to the necessary limitations in the number of hymns, dependent to a considerable degree upon the predetermined size and style of the book.

A noteworthy excellence is the conscientious care which has been taken to conform the text to the latest accredited sources of authority in hymnology.

The original illustrations from the brush of Mr. Harlow are a unique feature of this volume. His widely recognized worth as a landscape artist in water-colors will attract an interested attention to the sketches with which he has enriched the text. Many of them are sympathetic interpretations of the tone of feeling found at the heart of the accompanying poems. Some of them are expressions of moods of feeling induced by the sentiment of the hymns, and suggestive of certain aspects of external nature. Others are direct studies from nature, that have had for the artist a poetic value in the spirit of the visible scenes.

Introduction.

It is believed that the hymns collected in this little volume, representing ages of inspiration and devotion, will conspire with all that is true and beautiful and good in our common human nature, in helping, according to their measure, to make men wiser, purer, and happier.

J. W. CHURCHILL.

ANDOVER THEOLOGICAL SEMINARY,
October 25, 1892.

THE WORLD'S BEST HYMNS

Now we should praise
The Guardian of the Heavenly Kingdom;
The mighty Creator,
And the thoughts of His mind,
Glorious Father of His works!
As He, of every glory
Eternal Lord!
Established the beginning:
So He first shaped
The earth for the children of men,
And the Heav'ns for its canopy,
Holy Creator!
The middle region,
The Guardian of Mankind,
The Eternal Lord,
Afterwards made
The ground for men,
Almighty Ruler!

FROM ALFRED'S TRANSLATION OF BEDE.
(*Attributed to Cædmon. The earliest Anglo-Saxon hymn.*)

Gently, Lord.

GENTLY, Lord, oh, gently lead us,
    Pilgrims in this vale of tears,
    Through the trials yet decreed us,
Till our last great change appears.
When temptation's darts assail us,
    When in devious paths we stray,
Let Thy goodness never fail us,
    Lead us in Thy perfect way.

In the hour of pain and anguish,
    In the hour when death draws near,
Suffer not our hearts to languish,
    Suffer not our souls to fear ;
And, when mortal life is ended,
    Bid us in Thine arms to rest,
Till, by angel bands attended,
    We awake among the blest.

THOMAS HASTINGS.

Light shining out of Darkness.

GOD moves in a mysterious way,
   His wonders to perform;
He plants His footsteps in the sea,
   And rides upon the storm.

Deep in unfathomable mines
   Of never-failing skill
He treasures up His bright designs,
   And works His sovereign will.

Ye fearful saints, fresh courage take;
   The clouds ye so much dread
Are big with mercy, and shall break
   In blessings on your head.

Judge not the Lord by feeble sense.
   But trust Him for His grace;
Behind a frowning Providence
   He hides a smiling face.

2

His purposes will ripen fast,
   Unfolding every hour ;
The bud may have a bitter taste,
   But sweet will be the flower.

Blind unbelief is sure to err,
   And scan His work in vain ;
God is His own interpreter,
   And He will make it plain.

WILLIAM COWPER.

3

Jesu, Lover of my Soul.

JESU, Lover of my soul,
   Let me to Thy bosom fly,
While the nearer waters roll,
   While the tempest still is high !
Hide me, O my Saviour, hide,
   Till the storm of life is past,
Safe into the haven guide ;
   Oh. receive my soul at last !

Other refuge have I none ;
   Hangs my helpless soul on Thee ;
Leave, ah ! leave me not alone,
   Still support and comfort me !
All my trust on Thee is stayed,
   All my help from Thee I bring ;
Cover my defenceless head
   With the shadow of Thy wing !

4

Wilt Thou not regard my call?
  Wilt Thou not accept my prayer?
Lo! I sink, I faint, I fall!
  Lo! on thee I cast my care!
Reach me out Thy gracious hand!
  While I of Thy strength receive,
Hoping against hope I stand,
  Dying, and behold I live!

Thou, O Christ, art all I want;
  More than all in Thee I find;
Raise the fallen, cheer the faint,
  Heal the sick, and lead the blind!
Just and holy is Thy Name,
  I am all unrighteousness;
False and full of sin I am,
  Thou art full of truth and grace.

Plenteous grace with Thee is found, —
  Grace to cover all my sin;
Let the healing streams abound;
  Make and keep me pure within!
Thou of Life the Fountain art,
  Freely let me take of thee!
Spring Thou up within my heart!
  Rise to all eternity!

5   CHARLES WESLEY.

Watchman, tell us of the Night.

WATCHMAN, tell us of the night,
    What its signs of promise are !
    Traveller, o'er yon mountain's height
See that glory-beaming star !
Watchman, does its beauteous ray
    Aught of hope or joy foretell?
Traveller, yes ; it brings the day,
    Promised day of Israel.

Watchman, tell us of the night, —
    Higher yet that star ascends !
Traveller, blessedness and light,
    Peace and truth, its course portends.
Watchman, will its beams alone
    Gild the spot that gave them birth?
Traveller, ages are its own, —
    See, it bursts o'er all the earth !

Watchman, tell us of the night,
　For the morning seems to dawn.
Traveller, darkness takes its flight,
　Doubt and terror are withdrawn.
Watchman, let thy wanderings cease ;
　Hie thee to thy quiet home.
Traveller, lo ! the Prince of Peace,
　Lo ! the Son of God, is come.

SIR JOHN BOWRING.

7

While Shepherds watched.

WHILE shepherds watched their flocks by night,
    All seated on the ground,
The angel of the Lord came down,
    And glory shone around.

" Fear not," said he (for mighty dread
    Had seized their troubled mind) ;
" Glad tidings of great joy I bring
    To you and all mankind.

" To you, in David's town, this day
    Is born of David's line
The Saviour who is Christ the Lord :
    And this shall be the sign :

" The heavenly Babe you there shall find
    To human view displayed,
All meanly wrapt in swathing bands,
    And in a manger laid."

8

Thus spake the seraph ; and forthwith
   Appeared a shining throng
Of angels, praising God, and thus
   Addressed their joyful song :

" All glory be to God on high,
   And to the earth be peace ;
Good will henceforth from heaven to men
   Begin, and never cease ! "

NAHUM TATE.

9

It came upon the Midnight Clear.

IT came upon the midnight clear,
   That glorious song of old,
From angels bending near the earth
   To touch their harps of gold :
" Peace on the earth, good will to men
   From Heaven's all-gracious King ! "
The world in solemn stillness lay
   To hear the angels sing.

Still through the cloven skies they come,
   With peaceful wings unfurled ;
And still their heavenly music floats
   O'er all the weary world :
Above its sad and lowly plains
   They bend on hovering wing,
And ever o'er its Babel sounds
   The blessed angels sing.

But with the woes of sin and strife
  The world has suffered long ;
Beneath the angel strain have rolled
  Two thousand years of wrong ;
And man, at war with man, hears not
  The love-song which they bring.
Oh, hush the noise, ye men of strife,
  And hear the angels sing !

And ye, beneath life's crushing load
  Whose forms are bending low,
Who toil along the climbing way
  With painful steps and slow,
Look now ! for glad and golden hours
  Come swiftly on the wing ;
Oh, rest beside the weary road,
  And hear the angels sing !

For, lo ! the days are hastening on,
  By prophet bards foretold,
When with the ever-circling years
  Comes round the age of gold ;
When peace shall over all the earth
  Its ancient splendors fling,
And the whole world send back the song
  Which now the angels sing.

Edmund H. Sears.

11

Shout the Glad Tidings.

HOUT the glad tidings, exultingly sing;
 Jerusalem triumphs, Messiah is King!

Sion, the marvellous story be telling.
 The Son of the Highest, how lowly his birth!
The brightest archangel in glory excelling,
 He stoops to redeem thee, he reigns upon earth.
 Shout the glad tidings, exultingly sing:
 Jerusalem triumphs, Messiah is King!

Tell how He cometh; from nation to nation,
 The heart-cheering news let the earth echo round:
How free to the faithful He offers salvation,
 How His people with joy everlasting are crowned.
 Shout the glad tidings, exultingly sing;
 Jerusalem triumphs, Messiah is King!

12

Shout the Glad Tidings.

Mortals, your homage be gratefully bringing,
   And sweet let the gladsome hosanna arise ;
Ye angels, the full hallelujah be singing ;
   One chorus resound through the earth and the skies.
     Shout the glad tidings, exultingly sing ;
     Jerusalem triumphs, Messiah is King !

WILLIAM AUGUSTUS MUHLENBERG.

13

𝕳𝖆𝖗𝖐, 𝖙𝖍𝖊 𝕲𝖑𝖆𝖉 𝕾𝖔𝖚𝖓𝖉!

ARK, the glad sound! the Saviour comes,
 The Saviour promised long;
Let every heart prepare a throne,
 And every voice a song!

On Him the Spirit, largely poured,
 Exerts his sacred fire;
Wisdom and might, and zeal and love,
 His holy breast inspire.

He comes, the prisoners to release
 In Satan's bondage held;
The gates of brass before Him burst,
 The iron fetters yield.

He comes, from thickest films of vice
 To clear the mental ray,
And on the eyeballs of the blind
 To pour celestial day.

14

He comes, the broken heart to bind,
  The bleeding soul to cure,
And with the treasures of His grace
  To enrich the humble poor.

His silver trumpets publish loud
  The jubilee of the Lord ;
Our debts are all remitted now,
  Our heritage restored.

Our glad hosannas, Prince of Peace,
  Thy welcome shall proclaim,
And heaven's eternal arches ring
  With thy belovéd name.

Philip Doddridge.

Epiphany.

RIGHTEST and best of the sons of the morning,
   Dawn on our darkness, and lend us Thine aid !
Star of the East, the horizon adorning,
   Guide where our infant Redeemer is laid !

Cold on His cradle the dewdrops are shining,
   Low lies his head with the beasts of the stall ;
Angels adore Him, in slumber reclining,—
   Maker, and Monarch, and Saviour of all.

Say, shall we yield Him, in costly devotion,
   Odors of Edom. and offerings divine,
Gems of the mountain, and pearls of the ocean,
   Myrrh from the forest, or gold from the mine ?

Vainly we offer each ample oblation,
   Vainly with gifts would His favor secure ;
Richer by far is the heart's adoration,
   Dearer to God are the prayers of the poor.

Brightest and best of the sons of the morning,
    Dawn on our darkness, and lend us Thine aid !
Star of the East, the horizon adorning,
    Guide where our infant Redeemer is laid !

REGINALD HEBER.

17

Gethsemane.

G O to dark Gethsemane,
    Ye that feel the tempter's power;
Your Redeemer's conflict see,
    Watch with Him one bitter hour;
Turn not from His griefs away,
Learn of Jesus Christ to pray!

Follow to the judgment hall,
    View the Lord of life arraigned;
O the wormwood and the gall!
    O the pangs his soul sustained!
Shun not suffering, shame, or loss, —
Learn of Him to bear the cross!

Calvary's mournful mountain climb;
    There, adoring at His feet,
Mark that miracle of time,
    God's own sacrifice complete!
" It is finished!" — hear the cry;
Learn of Jesus Christ to die!

Early hasten to the tomb
  Where they laid His breathless clay ;
All is solitude and gloom ;
  Who hath taken Him away?
Christ is risen !   He meets our eyes !
Saviour, teach us so to rise !

JAMES MONTGOMERY.

19

Coronation.

LL hail the power of Jesus' name!
    Let angels prostrate fall;
Bring forth the royal diadem,
    To crown Him Lord of all!

Let high-born seraphs tune the lyre,
    And, as they tune it, fall
Before His face who tunes their choir,
    And crown Him Lord of all!

Crown Him, ye morning stars of light,
    Who fixed this floating ball;
Now hail the Strength of Israel's might,
    And crown Him Lord of all!

Crown Him, ye martyrs of your God,
    Who from His altar call;
Extol the stem of Jesse's rod,
    And crown Him Lord of all!

Ye seed of Israel's chosen race,
  Ye ransomed of the fall,
Hail Him who saves you by His grace,
  And crown Him Lord of all!

Hail Him, ye heirs of David's line,
  Whom David Lord did call,
The God incarnate, Man divine,
  And crown Him Lord of all!

Sinners, whose love can ne'er forget
  The wormwood and the gall,
Go spread your trophies at His feet,
  And crown Him Lord of all!

Let every tribe and every tongue
  That bound creations call
Now shout, in universal song,
  THE CROWNÉD LORD OF ALL!

              EDWARD PERRONET.

Hail to the Lord's Anointed.

AIL to the Lord's Anointed,
   Great David's greater Son!
Hail, in the time appointed,
   His reign on earth begun!
He comes to break oppression,
   To let the captive free,
To take away transgression,
   And rule in equity.

He comes with succor speedy
   To those who suffer wrong;
To help the poor and needy,
   And bid the weak be strong;
To give them songs for sighing,
   Their darkness turn to light,
Whose souls, condemned and dying,
   Were precious in His sight.

22

He shall come down like showers
  Upon the fruitful earth,
And love, joy, hope, like flowers,
  Spring in His path to birth.
Before Him, on the mountains,
  Shall Peace, the herald, go,
And righteousness, in fountains,
  From hill to valley flow.

Arabia's desert-ranger
  To Him shall bow the knee ;
The Ethiopian stranger
  His glory come to see ;
With offerings of devotion
  Ships from the isles shall meet,
To pour the wealth of ocean
  In tribute at His feet.

Kings shall fall down before Him,
  And golden incense bring ;
All nations shall adore Him,
  His praise all people sing ;
For He shall have dominion
  O'er river, sea, and shore,
Far as the eagle's pinion
  Or dove's light wing can soar.

Hail to the Lord's Anointed.

For Him shall prayer unceasing
  And daily vows ascend,
His kingdom still increasing.
  A kingdom without end ;
The mountain dews shall nourish
  A seed, in weakness sown.
Whose fruit shall spread and flourish,
  And shake like Lebanon.

O'er every foe victorious
  He on His throne shall rest,
From age to age more glorious,
  All-blessing and all-blest ;
The tide of time shall never
  His covenant remove :
His Name shall stand forever, —
  That Name to us is Love.

JAMES MONTGOMERY

Before Jehovah's awful Throne.

EFORE Jehovah's awful throne,
    Ye nations, bow with sacred joy ;
Know that the Lord is God alone,
    He can create, and He destroy.

His sovereign power, without our aid,
    Make us of clay, and formed us men ;
And when like wandering sheep we strayed,
    He brought us to His fold again.

We 'll crowd Thy gates with thankful songs,
    High as the heavens our voices raise ;
And earth, with her ten thousand tongues,
    Shall fill Thy courts with sounding praise.

Wide as the world is Thy command,
    Vast as eternity Thy love ;
Firm as a rock Thy truth must stand,
    When rolling years shall cease to move.

ISAAC WATTS.
(Varied by CHARLES WESLEY.)

God is Love.

OD is love !   His mercy brightens
All the path in which we rove ;
Bliss He wakes, and woe He lightens :
God is wisdom ! God is love !

Chance and change are busy ever ;
Man decays, and ages move ;
But His mercy waneth never :
God is wisdom ! God is love !

E'en the hour that darkest seemeth
Will His changeless goodness prove ;
From the gloom His brightness streameth :
God is wisdom ! God is love !

He with earthly cares entwineth
Hope and comfort from above ;
Everywhere His glory shineth :
God is wisdom ! God is love !

God is Love.

God is love! His mercy brightens
   All the path in which we rove ;
Bliss He wakes, and woe He lightens :
   God is wisdom ! God is love !

               Sir John Bowring.

The Holy Trinity.

HOLY, holy, holy, Lord God Almighty !
Early in the morning our songs shall rise to
Thee ;
Holy, holy, holy ! Merciful and Mighty !
God in Three Persons, blessed Trinity !

Holy, holy, holy ! all the saints adore Thee,
Casting down their golden crowns around the glassy
sea.
Cherubim and seraphim falling down before Thee,
Which wert, and art, and evermore shalt be.

Holy, holy, holy ! though the darkness hide Thee,
Though the eye of sinful man Thy glory may not
see.
Only Thou art holy, there is none beside Thee.
Perfect in power, in love, and purity.

28

The Holy Trinity.

Holy, holy, holy, Lord God Almighty!
   All Thy works shall praise Thy Name in earth and
      sky and sea;
Holy, holy, holy! Merciful and Mighty!
   God in Three Persons, blessed Trinity!

REGINALD HEBER.

When all thy Mercies, O my God.

HEN all Thy mercies, O my God,
My rising soul surveys,
Transported with the view, I 'm lost
In wonder, love, and praise.

Oh, how shall words with equal warmth
The gratitude declare
That glows within my ravished heart?
But Thou canst read it there.

Thy providence my life sustained,
And all my wants redressed,
When in the silent womb I lay,
And hung upon the breast.

To all my weak complaints and cries
Thy mercy lent an ear,
Ere yet my feeble thoughts had learnt
To form themselves in prayer.

30

When all Thy Mercies, O my God.

Unnumbered comforts on my soul
　　Thy tender care bestowed,
Before my infant heart conceived
　　From whence these comforts flowed.

When in the slippery paths of youth
　　With heedless steps I ran,
Thine arm, unseen, conveyed me safe,
　　And led me up to man.

Through hidden dangers, toils, and death
　　It gently cleared my way,
And through the pleasing snares of vice,
　　More to be feared than they.

When worn with sickness, oft hast Thou
　　With health renewed my face,
And when in sins and sorrows sunk,
　　Revived my soul with grace.

Thy bounteous hand with worldly bliss
　　Has made my cup run o'er,
And in a kind and faithful friend
　　Has doubled all my store.

Ten thousand thousand precious gifts
　　My daily thanks employ,
Nor is the least a cheerful heart,
　　That tastes those gifts with joy.

Through every period of my life
　　Thy goodness I 'll pursue,
And after death, in distant worlds,
　　The glorious theme renew.

When Nature fails, and day and night
　　Divide Thy works no more,
My ever grateful heart, O Lord,
　　Thy mercy shall adore.

Through all eternity to Thee
　　A joyful song I 'll raise ;
But oh ! eternity 's too short
　　To utter all Thy praise !

　　　　　　　　　JOSEPH ADDISON.

32

Psalm CXVII.

FROM all that dwell below the skies
  Let the Creator's praise arise ;
  Let the Redeemer's Name be sung
Through every land, by every tongue !

Eternal are Thy mercies, Lord ;
Eternal truth attends Thy word ;
Thy praise shall sound from shore to shore,
Till suns shall rise and set no more.

ISAAC WATTS

33

Praise to God.

PRAISE to God, immortal praise,
　　For the love that crowns our days !
　　Bounteous Source of every joy,
Let Thy praise our tongues employ.

For the blessings of the field,
For the stores the gardens yield.
For the vine's exalted juice,
For the generous olive's use, —

Flocks that whiten all the plain,
Yellow sheaves of ripened grain,
Clouds that drop their fattening dews,
Suns that temperate warmth diffuse, —

All that Spring with bounteous hand
Scatters o'er the smiling land,
All that liberal Autumn pours
From her rich, o'erflowing stores, —

34

Praise to God.

These to Thee, my God, we owe,
Source whence all our blessings flow,
And for these my soul shall raise
Grateful vows and solemn praise.

Yet, should rising whirlwinds tear
From its stem the ripening ear ;
Should the fig-tree's blasted shoot
Drop her green, untimely fruit ;

Should the vine put forth no more,
Nor the olive yield her store ;
Though the sickening flocks should fall,
And the herds desert the stall ;

Should Thine altered hand restrain
The early and the latter rain,
Blast each opening bud of joy,
And the rising year destroy, —

Yet to Thee my soul should raise
Grateful vows and solemn praise ;
And, when every blessing 's flown,
Love Thee for Thyself alone !

Anna Lætitia Barbauld.

Behold, I stand at the Door and knock.

O JESU, Thou art standing
    Outside the fast-closed door,
In lowly patience waiting
    To pass the threshold o'er.
We bear the name of Christians,
    His name and sign we bear ;
O shame, thrice shame upon us,
    To keep Him standing there !

O Jesu, thou art knocking,
    And lo! that hand is scarred,
And thorns Thy brow encircle,
    And tears Thy face have marred.
O love that passeth knowledge,
    So patiently to wait !
O sin that hath no equal,
    So fast to bar the gate !

36

Behold, I stand at the Door and knock.

O Jesu, Thou art pleading,
  In accents meek and low,
" I died for you, my children,
  And will ye treat me sᵣ ? "
O Lord, with shame and sorrow
  We open now the door !
Dear Saviour, enter, enter,
  And leave us nevermore !

WILLIAM WALSHAM HOW.

37

My Faith looks up to Thee.

Y faith looks up to Thee,
　　Thou Lamb of Calvary,
　　　Saviour divine!
Now hear me while I pray:
Take all my guilt away;
Oh, let me from this day
　　Be wholly thine!

May Thy rich grace impart
Strength to my fainting heart,
　　My zeal inspire!
As Thou hast died for me,
Oh, may my love to Thee
Pure, warm, and changeless be,
　　A living fire!

While life's dark maze I tread,
And griefs around me spread,
　　Be Thou my Guide!

Bid darkness turn to day,
Wipe sorrow's tears away,
Nor let me ever stray
  From Thee aside.

When ends life's transient dream,
When death's cold, sullen stream
  Shall o'er me roll,
Blest Saviour, then in love
Fear and distrust remove !
Oh, bear me safe above,
  A ransomed soul !

RAY PALMER.

Jesus, I my Cross have taken.

JESUS, I my cross have taken,
　　All to leave, and follow Thee ;
Destitute, despised, forsaken,
　　Thou from hence my all shalt be ;
Perish every fond ambition,
　　All I 've sought, or hoped, or known ;
Yet how rich is my condition !
　　God and heaven are still my own !

Let the world despise and leave me,
　　They have left my Saviour too ;
Human hearts and looks deceive me ;
　　Thou art not, like them, untrue.
And, while Thou shalt smile upon me.
　　God of wisdom, love, and might,
Foes may hate and friends may shun me ;
　　Show thy face, and all is bright !

Jesus, I my Cross have taken.

Go, then, earthly fame and treasure !
  Come disaster, scorn, and pain !
In Thy service, pain is pleasure ;
  With Thy favor, loss is gain.
I have called Thee, Abba, Father !
  I have stayed my heart on Thee !
Storms may howl, and clouds may gather,
  All must work for good to me.

Man may trouble and distress me,
  'T will but drive me to Thy breast ;
Life with trials hard may press me,
  Heaven will bring me sweeter rest.
Oh, 't is not in grief to harm me,
  While Thy love is left to me !
Oh, 't were not in joy to charm me,
  Were that joy unmixed with Thee !

Take, my soul, thy full salvation ;
  Rise o'er sin, and fear, and care ;
Joy to find, in every station,
  Something still to do or bear.
Think what Spirit dwells within thee !
  What a Father's smile is thine !
What a Saviour died to win thee !
  Child of Heaven, shouldst thou repine ?

Haste, then, on from grace to glory,
  Armed by faith, and winged by prayer!
Heaven's eternal day 's before thee ;
  God's own hand shall guide thee there !
Soon shall close thy earthly mission,
  Swift shall pass thy pilgrim days,
Hope soon change to glad fruition,
  Faith to sight, and prayer to praise !

HENRY FRANCIS LYTE.

Softly now the Light of Day.

OFTLY now the light of day
   Fades upon my sight away ;
   Free from care, from labor free,
Lord, I would commune with Thee.

Thou, whose all-pervading eye
   Naught escapes, without, within,
Pardon each infirmity,
   Open fault, and secret sin.

Soon for me the light of day
Shall forever pass away ;
Then, from sin and sorrow free,
Take me, Lord, to dwell with thee.

Thou who, sinless, yet hast known
   All of man's infirmity,
Then, from Thine eternal throne,
   Jesus, look with pitying eye.

GEORGE WASHINGTON DOANE.

43

Rock of Ages.

ROCK of Ages. cleft for me,
  Let me hide myself in Thee !
  Let the water and the blood,
From Thy riven side which flowed,
Be of sin the double cure,
Cleanse me from its guilt and power.

Not the labors of my hands
Can fulfil Thy law's demands ;
Could my zeal no respite know,
Could my tears forever flow.
All for sin could not atone :
Thou must save, and Thou alone.

Nothing in my hand I bring ;
Simply to Thy Cross I cling ;
Naked, come to Thee for dress ;
Helpless. look to Thee for grace ;
Foul, I to the Fountain fly :
Wash me, Saviour. or I die.

Rock of Ages.

While I draw this fleeting breath,
When my eyestrings break in death,
When I soar through tracts unknown,
See Thee on Thy judgment throne, —
Rock of Ages, cleft for me,
Let me hide myself in Thee !

AUGUSTUS MONTAGUE TOPLADY

Abide with Me.

BIDE with me ! fast falls the eventide ;
  The darkness deepens ; Lord, with me abide !
  When other helpers fail, and comforts flee,
Help of the helpless, oh, abide with me !

Swift to its close ebbs out life's little day ;
Earth's joys grow dim ; its glories pass away ;
Change and decay in all around I see :
O Thou, who changest not, abide with me !

Not a brief glance I beg, a passing word,
But, as Thou dwell'st with Thy disciples, Lord,
Familiar, condescending, patient, free,
Come, not to sojourn, but abide with me !

Come not in terrors, as the King of kings,
But kind and good, with healing in Thy wings,
Tears for all woes, a heart for every plea,
Come, Friend of sinners, and thus 'bide with me !

Abide with Me.

Thou on my head in early youth didst smile ;
And, though rebellious and perverse meanwhile,
Thou hast not left me, oft as I left Thee.
On to the close, O Lord, abide with me !

I need Thy presence every passing hour ;
What but Thy grace can foil the tempter's power ?
Who like Thyself my guide and stay can be ?
Through cloud and sunshine, oh, abide with me !

I fear no foe with Thee at hand to bless ;
Ills have no weight, and tears no bitterness.
Where is Death's sting ? where, Grave, thy victory ?
I triumph still, if Thou abide with me !

Hold then Thy cross before my closing eyes ;
Shine through the gloom, and point me to the skies ;
Heaven's morning breaks, and earth's vain shadows
        flee ;
In life and death, O Lord, abide with me !

HENRY FRANCIS LYTE.

The Morning Light is breaking.

HE morning light is breaking.
   The darkness disappears.
The sons of earth are waking
   To penitential tears.
Each breeze that sweeps the ocean
   Brings tidings from afar
Of nations in commotion,
   Prepared for Zion's war.

Rich dews of grace come o'er us
   In many a gentle shower,
And brighter scenes before us
   Are opening every hour;
Each day, to Heaven going,
   Abundant answer brings,
And heavenly gales are blowing,
   With peace upon their wings.

48

See heathen nations bending
   Before the God we love,
And thousand hearts ascending
   In gratitude above ;
While sinners, now confessing,
   The gospel call obey,
And seek the Saviour's blessing,
   A nation in a day.

Blest river of salvation,
   Pursue thy onward way ;
Flow thou to every nation,
   Nor in thy richness stay ;
Stay not till all the lowly
   Triumphant reach their home ;
Stay not till all the holy
   Proclaim, " The Lord is come ! "

SAMUEL FRANCIS SMITH.

Nearer, my God, to Thee.

NEARER, my God, to Thee,
Nearer to Thee!
E'en though it be a cross
That raiseth me;
Still all my song shall be,
Nearer, my God, to Thee.
Nearer to Thee!

Though like the wanderer,
The sun gone down,
Darkness be over me,
My rest a stone.
Yet in my dreams I'd be
Nearer, my God, to Thee,
Nearer to Thee!

There let the way appear
Steps unto heaven;
All that Thou sendest me
In mercy given;

Angels to beckon me
Nearer, my God, to Thee,
  Nearer to Thee!

Then, with my waking thoughts
  Bright with Thy praise,
Out of my stony griefs
  Bethel I 'll raise ;
So by my woes to be
Nearer, my God, to Thee,
  Nearer to Thee!

Or if on joyful wing
  Cleaving the sky,
Sun, moon, and stars forgot,
  Upward I fly, —
Still all my song shall be,
Nearer, my God, to Thee,
  Nearer to Thee.

SARAH FLOWER ADAMS.

"Of such is the Kingdom of Heaven."

THINK, when I read that sweet story of old,
When Jesus was here among men,
How he called little children as lambs to his fold,
I should like to have been with them then.

I wish that His hands had been placed on my head,
That His arm had been thrown around me,
And that I might have seen His kind look when he said,
" Let the little ones come unto me."

Yet still to His footstool in prayer I may go,
And ask for a share in His love ;
And if I thus earnestly seek Him below,
I shall see Him and hear Him above,

In that beautiful place He has gone to prepare
For all who are washed and forgiven ;
And many dear children shall be with Him there,
For of such is the kingdom of heaven.

But thousands and thousands who wander and fall
  Never heard of that heavenly home ;
I wish they could know there is room for them all,
  And that Jesus had bid them to come.

I long for the joy of that glorious time,
  The sweetest, the brightest, the best,
When the dear little children of every clime
  Shall crowd to His arms and be blest.

JEMIMA THOMPSON LUKE.

53

Just as I am.

JUST as I am, without one plea,
But that Thy blood was shed for me,
And that Thou bidd'st me come to Thee.
O Lamb of God, I come !

Just as I am, and waiting not,
To rid my soul of one dark blot,
To Thee, whose blood can cleanse each spot,
O Lamb of God, I come !

Just as I am, though tossed about
With many a conflict, many a doubt,
Fightings and fears within, without,
O Lamb of God, I come !

Just as I am, poor, wretched, blind,
Sight, riches, healing of the mind,
Yea, all I need, in Thee to find,
O Lamb of God, I come !

Just as I am.

Just as I am, Thou wilt receive,
Wilt welcome, pardon, cleanse, relieve!
Because Thy promise I believe,
   O Lamb of God, I come!

Just as I am, — Thy love unknown
Has broken every barrier down, —
Now, to be Thine, yea, Thine alone,
   O Lamb of God, I come!

Just as I am, of that free love
The breadth, length, depth, and height to prove,
Here for a season, then above,
   O Lamb of God, I come!

CHARLOTTE ELLIOTT.

Whilst Thee I seek.

WHILST Thee I seek, protecting Power,
  Be my vain wishes stilled,
And may this consecrated hour
  With better hopes be filled!

Thy love the power of thought bestowed;
  To Thee my thoughts would soar;
Thy mercy o'er my life has flowed,
  That mercy I adore.

In each event of life, how clear
  Thy ruling hand I see!
Each blessing to my soul more dear
  Because conferred by Thee.

In every joy that crowns my days,
  In every pain I bear,
My heart shall find delight in praise,
  Or seek relief in prayer.

Whilst Thee I seek.

When gladness wings my favored hour
   Thy love my thoughts shall fill ;
Resigned, when storms of sorrow lower,
   My soul shall meet Thy will.

My lifted eye without a tear
   The gathering storm shall see ;
My steadfast heart shall know no fear,
   That heart shall rest on Thee.

HELEN MARIA WILLIAMS.

Guide me, O Thou great Jehovah!

GUIDE me, O Thou great Jehovah!
   Pilgrim through this barren land;
I am weak, but Thou art mighty;
   Hold me with Thy powerful hand.
      Bread of Heaven! Bread of Heaven!
      Feed me now and evermore.

Open now the crystal fountain,
   Whence the healing streams do flow;
Let the fiery, cloudy pillar
   Lead me all my journey through.
      Strong Deliverer! strong Deliverer!
      Be thou still my Strength and Shield.

When I tread the verge of Jordan,
   Bid my anxious fears subside;
Death of deaths, and hell's destruction,
   Land me safe on Canaan's side;
      Songs of praises, songs of praises,
      I will ever give to Thee.

Musing on my habitation,
  Musing on my heavenly home,
Fills my soul with holy longing.
  Come, my Jesus, quickly come !
    Vanity is all I see ;
    Lord, I long to be with Thee !

                WILLIAM WILLIAMS.

59

Early Piety.

B Y cool Siloam's shady rill
    How sweet the lily grows!
How sweet the breath beneath the hill
    Of Sharon's dewy rose!
Lo! such the child whose early feet
    The paths of peace have trod,
Whose secret heart with influence sweet
    Is upward drawn to God.

By cool Siloam's shady rill
    The lily must decay;
The rose that blooms beneath the hill
    Must shortly fade away;
And soon, too soon, the wintry hour
    Of man's maturer age
Will shake the soul with sorrow's power
    And stormy passion's rage.

Early Piety.

O Thou, whose infant feet were found
  Within Thy Father's shrine,
Whose years with changeless virtue crowned
  Were all alike divine,
Dependent on Thy bounteous breath,
  We seek Thy grace alone,
In childhood, manhood, age, and death
  To keep us still Thine own.

REGINALD HEBER.

Missionary Hymn.

FROM Greenland's icy mountains,
    From India's coral strand,
Where Afric's sunny fountains
    Roll down their golden sand,
From many an ancient river,
    From many a palmy plain,
They call us to deliver
    Their land from error's chain.

What though the spicy breezes
    Blow soft o'er Ceylon's isle, —
Though every prospect pleases,
    And only man is vile?
In vain with lavish kindness
    The gifts of God are strewn ;
The heathen in his blindness
    Bows down to wood and stone.

62

Can we, whose souls are lighted
   With wisdom from on high,
Can we to men benighted
   The lamp of life deny?
Salvation, O Salvation!
   The joyful sound proclaim,
Till each remotest nation
   Has learnt Messiah's Name.

Waft, waft, ye winds, His story,
   And you, ye waters, roll,
Till like a sea of glory
   It spreads from pole to pole;
'Till o'er our ransomed nature
   The Lamb for sinners slain,
Redeemer, King, Creator,
   In bliss returns to reign.

REGINALD HEBER.

𝕴 would not live Alway.

I WOULD not live alway, — live alway below!
Oh, no, I 'll not linger, when bidden to go.
The days of our pilgrimage granted us here
Are enough for life's woes, full enough for its cheer.
Would I shrink from the path which the prophets of
　　God,
Apostles, and martyrs so joyfully trod?
While brethren and friends are all hastening home,
Like a spirit unblest, o'er the earth would I roam?

I would not live alway: I ask not to stay
Where storm after storm rises dark o'er the way;
Where, seeking for rest, I but hover around
Like the patriarch's bird, and no resting is found;
Where Hope, when she paints her gay bow in the air,
Leaves her brilliance to fade in the night of despair,
And Joy's fleeting angel ne'er sheds a glad ray,
Save the gleam of the plumage that bears him away.

I would not live Alway.

I would not live alway, thus fettered by sin,
Temptation without, and corruption within ;
In a moment of strength, if I sever the chain,
Scarce the victory is mine ere I 'm captive again.
E'en the rapture of pardon is mingled with fears,
And the cup of thanksgiving with penitent tears.
The festival trump calls for jubilant songs,
But my spirit her own miserere prolongs.

I would not live alway : no, welcome the tomb !
Immortality's lamp burns there bright 'mid the gloom.
There, too, is the pillow where Christ bowed His head ;
Oh, soft be my slumbers on that holy bed !
And then the glad morn soon to follow that night,
When the sunrise of glory shall burst on my sight,
And the full matin-song, as the sleepers arise
To shout in the morning, shall peal through the skies.

Who, who would live alway, away from his God,
Away from yon heaven, that blissful abode,
Where the rivers of pleasure flow o'er the bright plains,
And the noontide of glory eternally reigns ;
Where the saints of all ages in harmony meet,
Their Saviour and brethren transported to greet,
While the anthems of rapture unceasingly roll,
And the smile of the Lord is the feast of the soul?

I would not live Alway.

That heavenly music! what is it I hear?
The notes of the harpers ring sweet on my ear.
And see soft unfolding those portals of gold,
The King, all arrayed in His beauty, behold!
Oh, give me, oh, give me the wings of a dove!
Let me hasten my flight to those mansions above!
Ay, 't is now that my soul on swift pinions would soar,
And in ecstasy bid earth adieu evermore.

WILLIAM AUGUSTUS MUHLENBERG.

Lead, Kindly Light.

LEAD, kindly Light, amid the encircling gloom,
  Lead Thou me on.
 The night is dark, and I am far from home ;
  Lead Thou me on ;
Keep Thou my feet ; I do not ask to see
The distant scene ; one step enough for me.

I was not ever thus, nor prayed that Thou
  Shouldst lead me on ;
I loved to choose and see my path ; but now
  Lead Thou me on.
I loved the garish day, and, spite of fears,
Pride ruled my will. Remember not past years !

So long Thy power has blest me, sure it still
  Will lead me on
O'er moor and fen, o'er crag and torrent, till
  The night is gone,
And with the morn those angel faces smile
Which I have loved long since, and lost awhile !

JOHN HENRY NEWMAN

There is a Happy Land.

THERE is a happy land,
Far, far away,
Where saints in glory stand,
Bright, bright as day.
Oh, how they sweetly sing.
Worthy is our Saviour King!
Loud let his praises ring, —
Praise, praise for aye !

Come to this happy land.
Come, come away ;
Why will ye doubting stand,
Why still delay?
Oh, we shall happy be,
When, from sin and sorrow free,
Lord, we shall live with Thee,
Blest, blest for aye.

68

There is a Happy Land.

Bright in that happy land
 Beams every eye ;
Kept by a Father's hand,
 Love cannot die.
On, then, to glory run ;
Be a crown and kingdom won ;
And, bright above the sun,
 Reign, reign for aye.

ANDREW YOUNG

There is a Land of Pure Delight.

HERE is a land of pure delight,
　　Where saints immortal reign,
　Infinite day excludes the night,
　　And pleasures banish pain.

There everlasting spring abides,
　And never-withering flowers ;
Death, like a narrow sea, divides
　This heavenly land from ours.

Sweet fields beyond the swelling flood
　Stand dressed in living green :
So to the Jews old Canaan stood,
　While Jordan rolled between.

But timorous mortals start and shrink
　To cross this narrow sea,
And linger shivering on the brink,
　And fear to launch away.

There is a Land of Pure Delight.

Oh, could we make our doubts remove,
    These gloomy doubts that rise,
And see the Canaan that we love
    With unbeclouded eyes, —

Could we but climb where Moses stood,
    And view the landscape o'er, —
Not Jordan's stream nor death's cold flood
    Should fright us from the shore !

                    ISAAC WATTS.

The Pilgrims of the Night.

ARK ! hark, my soul ! angelic songs are swelling
    O'er earth's green fields and ocean's wave-
       beat shore.
How sweet the truth those blessed strains are telling
   Of that new life, when sin shall be no more !
       Angels of Jesus,
        Angels of light.
       Singing to welcome
        The pilgrims of the night !

Darker than night life's shadows fall around us,
   And like benighted men we miss our mark :
God hides Himself, and grace hath scarcely found us,
   Ere death finds out his victims in the dark.
       Angels of Jesus,
        Angels of light,
       Singing to welcome
        The pilgrims of the night !

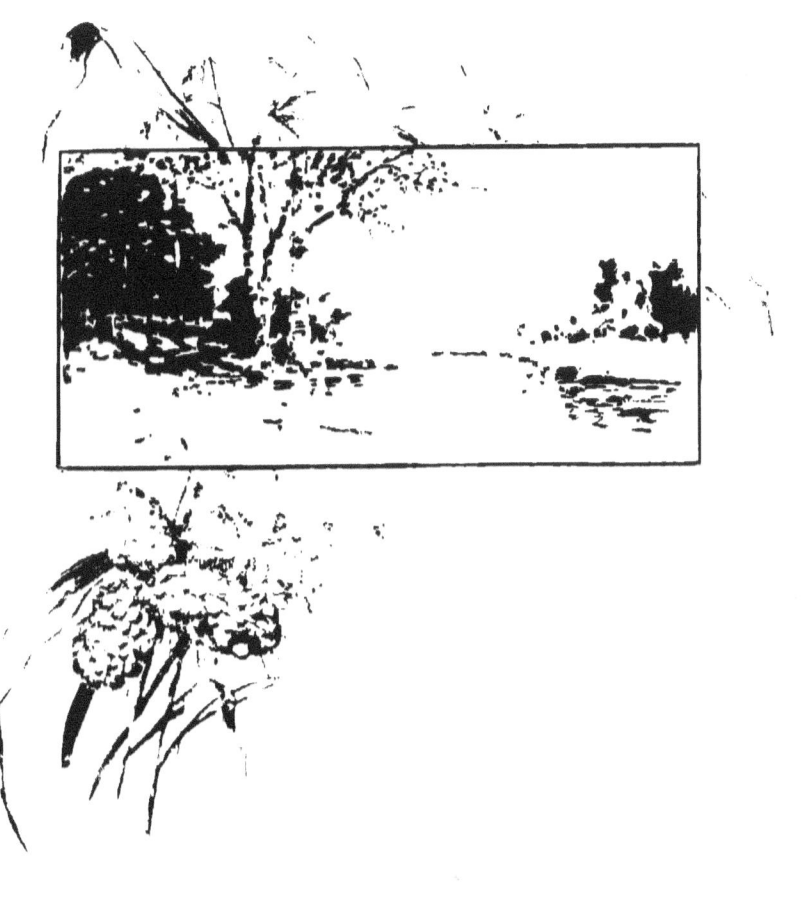

The Pilgrims of the Night.

Onward we go, for still we hear them singing,
  "Come, weary souls, for Jesus bids you come!"
And through the dark, its echoes sweetly ringing,
  The music of the Gospel leads us home.
        Angels of Jesus,
          Angels of light,
       Singing to welcome
         The pilgrims of the night!

Far, far away, like bells at evening pealing,
  The voice of Jesus sounds o'er land and sea;
And laden souls by thousands meekly stealing,
  Kind Shepherd, turn their weary steps to Thee.
        Angels of Jesus,
          Angels of light,
       Singing to welcome
         The pilgrims of the night!

Rest comes at last; though life be long and dreary,
  The day must dawn, and darksome night be past;
All journeys end in welcomes to the weary,
  And heaven, the heart's true home, will come at last.
        Angels of Jesus,
          Angels of light,
       Singing to welcome
         The pilgrims of the night!

The Pilgrims of the Night.

Cheer up, my soul! faith's moonbeams softly glisten
    Upon the breast of life's most troubled sea,
And it will cheer thy drooping heart to listen
    To those brave songs which angels mean for thee.
        Angels of Jesus,
          Angels of light,
        Singing to welcome
          The pilgrims of the night!

Angels, sing on, your faithful watches keeping,
    Sing us sweet fragments of the songs above,
While we toil on, and soothe ourselves with weeping,
    Till life's long night shall break in endless love.
        Angels of Jesus,
          Angels of light,
        Singing to welcome
          The pilgrims of the night!

FREDERICK WILLIAM FABER.

Lord, dismiss us, with Thy Blessing.

LORD, dismiss us, with Thy blessing ;
    Fill our hearts with joy and peace ;
    Let us each, Thy love possessing,
Triumph in redeeming grace ;
    Oh, refresh us,
    Travelling through this wilderness !

Thanks we give, and adoration,
    For Thy Gospel's joyful sound ;
May the fruit of Thy salvation
    In our hearts and lives abound !
    May thy presence
    With us evermore be found !

So, whene'er the signal 's given
    Us from earth to call away,
Borne on angels' wings to heaven,
    Glad the summons to obey,
    May we ever
    Reign with Christ in endless day !

75

Paradise.

PARADISE! O Paradise
   Who doth not crave for rest?
Who would not seek the happy land
   Where they that loved are blest?
Where loyal hearts and true
   Stand ever in the light,
All rapture through and through,
   In God's most holy sight?

O Paradise ! O Paradise !
   The world is growing old ;
Who would not be at rest and free
   Where love is never cold?
Where loyal hearts and true
   Stand ever in the light,
All rapture through and through,
   In God's most holy sight?

Paradise.

O Paradise! O Paradise!
Wherefore doth death delay, —
Bright death, that is the welcome dawn
Of our eternal day,
Where loyal hearts and true
Stand ever in the light,
All rapture through and through,
In God's most holy sight?

O Paradise! O Paradise!
'T is weary waiting here:
I long to be where Jesus is,
To feel, to see Him near,
Where loyal hearts and true
Stand ever in the light,
All rapture through and through,
In God's most holy sight.

O Paradise! O Paradise!
I want to sin no more;
I want to be as pure on earth
As on thy spotless shore,
Where loyal hearts and true
Stand ever in the light,
All rapture through and through,
In God's most holy sight.

Paradise.

O Paradise ! O Paradise !
  I greatly long to see
The special place my dearest Lord
  Is destining for me,
    Where loyal hearts and true
      Stand ever in the light,
    All rapture through and through,
      In God's most holy sight.

FREDERICK WILLIAM FABER.

78

Children of the Heavenly King.

HILDREN of the heavenly King,
As we journey, sweetly sing;
Sing our Saviour's worthy praise,
Glorious in His works and ways.

We are travelling home to God,
In the way the fathers trod :
They are happy now, and we
Soon their happiness shall see.

Banished once, by sin betrayed,
Christ our Advocate was made ;
Pardoned now, no more we roam,
Christ conducts us to our home.

Lord, obediently we go,
Gladly leaving all below ;
Only Thou our Leader be,
And we still will follow Thee.

JOHN CENNICK.

79

To Truth.

O STAR of Truth, down shining
    Through clouds of doubt and fear,
I ask but 'neath your guidance
    My pathway may appear.
However long the journey,
    How hard soe'er it be,
Though I be lone and weary,
    Lead on, I 'll follow thee !

I know thy blessed radiance
    Can never lead astray,
However ancient custom
    May tread some other way.
E'en if through untrod deserts,
    Or over trackless sea,
Though I be lone and weary,
    Lead on, I 'll follow thee !

To Truth.

The bleeding feet of martyrs
    Thy toilsome road have trod :
But fires of human passion
    May light the way to God.
Then, though my feet should falter,
    While I thy beams can see,
Though I be lone and dreary,
    Lead on, I 'll follow thee !

Though loving friends forsake me,
    Or plead with me in tears, —
Though angry foes may threaten
    To shake my soul with fears, —
Still to my high allegiance
    I must not faithless be :
Through life or death, forever
    Lead on, I 'll follow thee !

MINOT J. SAVAGE.

Still, still with Thee.

STILL, still with Thee, when purple morning breaketh,
When the bird waketh, and the shadows flee :
Fairer than morning, lovelier than the daylight,
Dawns the sweet consciousness I am with **Thee.**

Alone with Thee, amid the mystic shadows,
The solemn hush of Nature newly born ;
Alone with Thee, in breathless adoration,
In the calm dew and freshness of the morn.

As in the dawning o'er the waveless ocean
The image of the morning star doth rest,
So in this stillness Thou beholdest only
Thine image in the waters of my breast.

Still, still with Thee, as to each new-born morning
A fresh and solemn splendor still is given ;
So doth this blessed consciousness, awaking,
Breathe each day nearness unto Thee and heaven.

Still, still with Thee.

When sinks the soul, subdued by toil, to slumber,
  Its closing eye looks up to Thee in prayer ;
Sweet the repose beneath Thy wings o'ershadowing,
  But sweeter still to wake and find Thee there.

So shall it be at last, in that bright morning,
  When the soul waketh, and the shadows flee ;
Oh ! in that hour, fairer than daylight's dawning,
  Shall rise the glorious thought, I am with Thee.

MRS. H. B. STOWE.

I was a Wandering Sheep.

I WAS a wandering sheep,
    I did not love the fold,
        I did not love my Shepherd's voice,
           I would not be controlled.
I was a wayward child,
    I did not love my home,
I did not love my Father's voice,
    I loved afar to roam.

The Shepherd sought His sheep,
    The Father sought His child ;
They followed me o'er vale and hill,
    O'er deserts waste and wild.
They found me nigh to death,
    Famished, and faint, and lone ;
They bound me with the bands of love :
    They saved the wandering one.

I was a Wandering Sheep.

Jesus my Shepherd is :
'T was He that loved my soul,
'T was He that washed me in His blood.
'T was He that made me whole ;
'T was He that sought the lost,
That found the wandering sheep ;
'T was He that brought me to the fold,
'T is He that still doth keep.

I was a wandering sheep,
I would not be controlled ;
But now I love my Shepherd's voice,
I love, I love the fold !
I was a wayward child ;
I once preferred to roam ;
But now I love my Father's voice. —
I love, I love His home !

HORATIUS BONAR.

In Heavenly Love abiding.

IN heavenly love abiding,
　　No change my heart shall fear,
And safe in such confiding,
　　For nothing changes here.
The storm may roar without me,
　　My heart may low be laid;
But God is round about me,
　　And can I be dismayed?

Wherever He may guide me,
　　No want shall turn me back;
My Shepherd is beside me,
　　And nothing can I lack.
His wisdom ever waketh,
　　His sight is never dim.
He knows the way He taketh,
　　And I will walk with Him.

86

Green pastures are before me,
  Which yet I have not seen ;
Bright skies will soon be o'er me,
  Where darkest clouds have been.
My hope I cannot measure,
  My path to life is free ;
My Saviour has my treasure,
  And He will walk with me.

ANNA L. WARING.

In the Cross of Christ I glory.

N the cross of Christ I glory,
    Towering o'er the wrecks of time ;
All the light of sacred story
    Gathers round its head sublime.

When the woes of life o'ertake me,
    Hopes deceive, and fears annoy,
Never shall the cross forsake me :
    Lo ! it glows with peace and joy.

When the sun of bliss is beaming
    Light and love upon my way,
From the cross the radiance streaming
    Adds new lustre to the day.

Bane and blessing, pain and pleasure,
    By the cross are sanctified :
Peace is there that knows no measure,
    Joys that through all time abide.

In the Cross of Christ I glory.

In the cross of Christ I glory,
  Towering o'er the wrecks of time ;
All the light of sacred story
  Gathers round its head sublime.

JOHN BOWRING

O Holy Saviour.

HOLY Saviour. Friend unseen,
The faint, the weak, on Thee may lean ;
Help me throughout life's varying scene
By faith to cling to Thee.

Blest with communion so divine,
Take what Thou wilt, shall I repine,
When, as the branches to the vine,
My soul may cling to Thee?

Far from her home, fatigued, oppressed,
Here she has found a place of rest,
An exile still, yet not unblest,
While she can cling to Thee.

What though the world deceitful prove,
And earthly friends and joys remove,
With patient, uncomplaining love,
Still would I cling to Thee.

Though faith and hope awhile be tried,
I ask not, need not, aught beside ;
How safe, how calm, how satisfied,
   The soul that clings to Thee !

Blest is my lot, whate'er befall ;
What can disturb me, who appall,
While as my strength, my rock, my all,
   Saviour, I cling to Thee ?

CHARLOTTE ELLIOTT

When J Survey the Wondrous Cross.

HEN I survey the wondrous Cross
   On which the Prince of Glory died,
My richest gain I count but loss,
   And pour contempt on all my pride.

Forbid it, Lord, that I should boast,
   Save in the Cross of Christ, my God:
All the vain things that charm me most,
   I sacrifice them to Thy Blood.

See, from His head, His hands, His feet,
   Sorrow and love flow mingled down!
Did e'er such love and sorrow meet,
   Or thorns compose a Saviour's crown?

Were the whole realm of nature mine,
   That were a tribute far too small;
Love so amazing, so divine,
   Demands my life, my soul, my all.

ISAAC WATTS.

Saviour, breathe an Evening Blessing.

AVIOUR, breathe an evening blessing.
    Ere repose our spirits seal ;
Sin and want we come confessing,
    Thou canst save, and Thou canst heal.

Though destruction walk around us,
    Though the arrow past us fly,
Angel-guards from Thee surround us ;
    We are safe, if Thou art nigh.

Though the night be dark and dreary,
    Darkness cannot hide from Thee ;
Thou art He who, never weary,
    Watchest where Thy people be.

Should swift death this night o'ertake us,
    And our couch become our tomb,
May the morn in heaven awake us,
    Clad in light and deathless bloom.

JAMES EDMESTON.

Welcome, Happy Morning!

ELCOME, happy morning!
  Age to age shall say,
Hell to-day is vanquished,
  Heaven is won to-day!
Lo, the dead is living,
  God forevermore!
Him, their true Creator,
  All his works adore.

Earth with joy confesses,
  Clothing her for spring,
All good gifts returned with
  Her returning King:
Bloom in every meadow,
  Leaves on every bough,
Speak His sorrows ended,
  Hail His triumph now.

Maker and Redeemer,
  Life and health of all,
Thou, from heaven beholding
  Human nature's fall,

Of the Father's Godhead
  True and only Son,
Manhood to deliver,
  Manhood didst put on.

Thou, of life the Author,
  Death didst undergo,
Tread the path of darkness,
  Saving strength to show.
Come, then, true and faithful.
  Now fulfil Thy word,
'T is Thine own third morning,
  Rise, my buried Lord!

Loose the souls long prisoned,
  Bound with Satan's chain :
All that now is fallen
  Raise to life again ;
Show Thy face in brightness,
  Bid the nations see,
Bring again our daylight :
  Day returns with Thee.

VENANTIUS FORTUNATUS (Tr. ELLERTON).

95

When Morning gilds the Skies.

HEN morning gilds the skies,
　My heart, awaking. cries,
　　May Jesus Christ be praised!
Alike at work and prayer
To Jesus I repair;
May Jesus Christ be praised!

To Thee, my God above,
I cry with glowing love,
May Jesus Christ be praised!
This song of sacred joy,
It never seems to cloy,
May Jesus Christ be praised!

Does sadness fill my mind?
A solace here I find,
May Jesus Christ be praised!
Or fades my earthly bliss?
My comfort still is this,
May Jesus Christ be praised!

96

When evil thoughts molest,
With this I shield my breast,
May Jesus Christ be praised!
The powers of darkness fear,
When this sweet chant they hear,
May Jesus Christ be praised!

When sleep her balm denies,
My silent spirit sighs,
May Jesus Christ be praised!
The night becomes as day,
When from the heart we say,
May Jesus Christ be praised!

Be this, while life is mine,
My canticle divine,
May Jesus Christ be praised!
Be this the eternal song
Through all the ages on,
May Jesus Christ be praised!

German, Tr. CASWALL.

Lovest Thou Me?

HARK, my soul! it is the Lord:
'T is thy Saviour, hear his word;
Jesus speaks, and speaks to thee:
"Say, poor sinner, lovest thou me?

"I delivered thee when bound,
And when bleeding, healed thy wound;
Sought thee wandering, set thee right,
Turned thy darkness into light.

"Can a woman's tender care
Cease towards the child she bare?
Yes, she may forgetful be,
Yet will I remember thee.

"Mine is an unchanging love,
Higher than the heights above;
Deeper than the depths beneath,
Free and faithful, strong as death.

98

"Thou shalt see my glory soon,
When the work of grace is done,
Partner of my throne shalt be : —
Say, poor sinner, lovest thou me?"

Lord, it is my chief complaint,
That my love is weak and faint ;
Yet I love Thee and adore :
Oh ! for grace to love Thee more !

WILLIAM COWPER.

99

Blest be the Tie that binds.

LEST be the tie that binds
    Our hearts in Jesus' love ;
The fellowship of Christian minds
    Is like to that above.

Before our Father's throne
    We pour united prayers ;
Our fears, our hopes, our aims, are one,
    Our comforts, and our cares.

We share our mutual woes,
    Our mutual burdens bear,
And often for each other flows
    The sympathizing tear.

When we at death must part,
    Not like the world's our pain ;
But one in Christ, and one in heart,
    We part to meet again.

From sorrow, toil, and pain,
And sin, we shall be free ;
And perfect love and friendship reign
Throughout eternity.

JOHN FAWCETT.

101

Fierce was the Wild Billow.

FIERCE was the wild billow,
    Dark was the night;
Oars labored heavily,
    Foam glimmered white;
Mariners trembled,
  Peril was nigh;
Then said the God of God,
    " Peace!   It is I."

Ridge of the mountain wave,
    Lower thy crest;
Wail of the tempest wind,
    Be thou at rest;
Peril can none be,
  Sorrow must fly,
Where saith the Light of light,
    " Peace!   It is I."

Jesus, Deliverer,
  Come Thou to me ;
Soothe Thou my voyaging
  Over life's sea.
Thou, when the storm of death
  Roars, sweeping by,
Whisper, O Truth of truth,
  " Peace !   It is I."

ST. ANATOLIUS (Tr. NEALE).

103

Hark! the Herald Angels sing.

ARK! the herald angels sing
    Glory to the new-born King!
    Peace on earth, and mercy mild,
God and sinners reconciled!
Joyful, all ye nations, rise,
Join the triumph of the skies;
With the angelic host proclaim,
Christ is born in Bethlehem!
    Hark! the herald angels sing
    Glory to the new-born King!

Christ, by highest heaven adored,
Christ, the everlasting Lord,
Late in time, behold him come,
Offspring of the Virgin's womb!
Veiled in flesh the Godhead see,
Hail the Incarnate Deity,
Pleased as Man with men to dwell,
Jesus, our Emmanuel!
    Hark! the herald angels sing
    Glory to the new-born King!

Hark! the Herald Angels sing.

Risen with healing in His wings,
Light and life to all He brings.
Hail, the Sun of Righteousness !
Hail, the heaven-born Prince of Peace !
Holy Father, Holy Son,
Holy Spirit, Three in One !
Glory, as of old, to Thee
Now and evermore shall be !
    Hark ! the herald angels sing
    Glory to the new-born King !

CHARLES WESLEY.

I heard the Voice of Jesus say.

HEARD the voice of Jesus say,
    "Come unto Me and rest;
Lay down, thou weary one, lay down
    Thy head upon My breast."
I came to Jesus as I was,
    All weary, worn, and sad;
I found in Him a resting place,
    And He has made me glad.

I heard the voice of Jesus say,
    "Behold, I freely give
The living water; thirsty one,
    Stoop down, and drink, and live."
I came to Jesus, and I drank
    Of that life-giving stream;
My thirst was quenched, my soul revived,
    And now I live in Him.

I heard the voice of Jesus say,
   " I am this dark world's Light ;
Look unto Me, thy morn shall rise,
   And all thy day be bright."
I looked to Jesus, and I found
   In Him my Star, my Sun ;
And in that Light of life I 'll walk
   Till travelling days are done.

HORATIUS BONAR.

Jerusalem, the Golden!

JERUSALEM, the golden!
    With milk and honey blest,
Beneath thy contemplation
    Sink heart and voice oppressed.
I know not, oh, I know not
    What joys await us there,
What radiancy of glory,
    What bliss beyond compare.

They stand, those halls of Zion,
    All jubilant with song,
And bright with many an angel,
    And all the martyr throng.
The Prince is ever in them,
    The daylight is serene ;
The pastures of the blessèd
    Are decked in glorious sheen.

Jerusalem, the Golden.

There is the throne of David,
   And there, from care released,
The shout of them that triumph,
   The song of them that feast ;
And they, who with their Leader
   Have conquered in the fight,
Forever and forever
   Are clad in robes of white.

O sweet and blessèd country,
   The home of God's elect !
O sweet and blessèd country,
   That eager hearts expect !
Jesus, in mercy bring us
   To that dear land of rest,
Who art, with God the Father,
   And Spirit, ever blest.

ST. BERNARD (Tr. NEALE).

A Charge to keep I have.

 CHARGE to keep i   e,
　　A God to glorify,
　A never-dying soul to save,
　　And fit it for the sky.

From youth to hoary age,
　My calling to fulfil,
Oh, may it all my powers engage
　To do my Master's will!

Arm me with jealous care
　As in Thy sight to live ;
And oh, Thy servant, Lord, prepare
　A strict account to give!

Help me to watch and pray,
　And on Thyself rely,
Assured, if I my trust betray,
　I shall forever die.

CHARLES WESLEY

Oh, could I speak the Matchless Worth.

H, could I speak the matchless worth,
Oh, could I sound the glories forth,
    Which in my Saviour shine,
I 'd soar and touch the heavenly strings,
And vie with Gabriel while he sings
    In notes almost divine.

I 'd sing the characters He bears,
And all the forms of love He wears,
    Exalted on His throne ;
In loftiest songs of sweetest praise,
I would, to everlasting days,
    Make all His glories known.

Oh, the delightful day will come
When my dear Lord will bring me home,
    And I shall see His face !
Then, with my Saviour, Brother, Friend,
A blest eternity I 'll spend,
    Triumphant in His grace.

SAMUEL MEDLEY.

Onward, Christian Soldiers.

ONWARD, Christian soldiers!
    Marching as to war.
    With the cross of Jesus
    Going on before.
Christ the Royal Master
    Leads against the foe ;
Forward into battle,
    See, his banners go.

At the sign of triumph,
    Satan's host doth flee.
On, then, Christian soldiers,
    On to victory !
Hell's foundations quiver
    At the shout of praise ;
Brothers, lift your voices,
    Loud your anthems raise !

Like a mighty army
    Moves the Church of God ;
Brothers, we are treading
    Where the saints have trod ;

Onward, Christian Soldiers!

We are not divided,
All one body we.
One in hope and doctrine,
One in charity.

Crowns and thrones may perish,
Kingdoms rise and wane,
But the Church of Jesus
Constant will remain.
Gates of hell can never
'Gainst that Church prevail;
We have Christ's own promise,
And that cannot fail.

Onward, then, ye people!
Join our happy throng;
Blend with ours your voices
In the triumph song!
Glory, laud, and honor
Unto Christ the King!
This through countless ages
Men and angels sing.

S. BARING-GOULD.

Our blest Redeemer, ere He breathed.

UR blest Redeemer, ere He breathed
His tender, last farewell,
A Guide, a Comforter, bequeathed,
With us to dwell.

He came in semblance of a dove,
With sheltering wings outspread,
The holy balm of peace and love
On earth to shed.

He came sweet influence to impart.
A gracious, willing Guest,
While He can find one humble heart
Wherein to rest.

And His that gentle voice we hear,
Soft as the breath of even,
That checks each thought, that calms each fear,
And speaks of heaven.

Our Blest Redeemer, ere He breathed.

And every virtue we possess,
   And every victory won,
And every thought of holiness
   Are His alone.

Spirit of purity and grace,
   Our weakness, pitying, see ;
Oh, make our hearts Thy dwelling-place,
   And meet for Thee !

Oh, praise the Father, praise the Son !
   Blest Spirit, praise to Thee !
All praise to God, the Three in One,
   The One in Three !

                              HARRIET AUBER.

Sun of my Soul, Thou Saviour dear.

SUN of my soul, Thou Saviour dear,
It is not night if Thou be near;
Oh, may no earth-born cloud arise
To hide Thee from Thy servant's eyes!

When the soft dews of kindly sleep
My weary eyelids gently steep,
Be my last thought how sweet to rest
Forever on my Saviour's breast!

Abide with me from morn till eve,
For without Thee I cannot live;
Abide with me when night is nigh,
For without Thee I dare not die.

If some poor wandering child of Thine
Have spurned to-day the voice divine,
Now, Lord, the gracious work begin;
Let him no more lie down in sin.

Watch by the sick ; enrich the poor
With blessings from Thy boundless store ;
Be every mourner's sleep to-night,
Like infant slumbers, pure and light.

Come near and bless us when we wake,
Ere through the world our way we take,
Till in the ocean of Thy love
We lose ourselves in heaven above.

J. KEBLE.

117

The Shadows of the Evening Hours.

THE shadows of the evening hours
    Fall from the darkening sky;
Upon the fragrance of the flowers
    The dews of evening lie.
Before Thy throne, O Lord of heaven,
    We kneel at close of day;
Look on Thy children from on high,
    And hear us while we pray.

The sorrows of Thy servants, Lord,
    Oh, do not Thou despise!
But let the incense of our prayers
    Before Thy mercy rise.
The brightness of the coming night
    Upon the darkness rolls;
With hopes of future glory chase
    The shadows on our souls.

The Shadows of the Evening Hours.

Slowly the rays of daylight fade ;
  So fade within our heart
The hopes in earthly love and joy
  That one by one depart ;
Slowly the bright stars, one by one,
  Within the heavens shine :
Give us, O Lord, fresh hopes in heaven,
  And trust in things divine.

Let peace, O Lord ! Thy peace, O God !
  Upon our souls descend ;
From midnight fears and perils Thou
  Our trembling hearts defend :
Give us a respite from our toil,
  Calm and subdue our woes ;
Through the long day we suffer, Lord,
  Oh, give us now repose !

ADELAIDE PROCTOR.

\

Hark! what mean those Holy Voices?

HARK! what mean those holy voices,
  Sweetly sounding through the skies?
Lo! the angelic host rejoices,
  Heavenly Alleluias rise.

Listen to the wondrous story,
  Which they chant in hymns of joy:
" Glory in the highest, glory!
  Glory be to God most high!

" Peace on earth, good will from heaven,
  Reaching far as man is found:
Souls redeemed and sins forgiven,
  Loud our golden harps shall sound.

" Christ is born, the great Anointed!
  Heaven and earth His praises sing!
Oh, receive whom God appointed
  For your Prophet, Priest, and King!

Hark! what mean those Holy Voices?

"Hasten, mortals, to adore Him!
  Learn His Name to magnify,
Till in heaven ye sing before Him,
  Glory be to God most high!"

JOHN CAWOOD

A few more Years shall roll.

FEW more years shall roll,
   A few more seasons come,
   And we shall be with those at rest,
   Asleep within the tomb :
   Then, O my Lord, prepare
   My soul for that great day ;
Oh, wash me in Thy precious Blood,
   And take my sins away !

   A few more suns shall set
   O'er these dark hills of time.
And we shall be where suns are not,
   A far serener clime :
   Then, O my Lord, prepare
   My soul for that blest day ;
Oh, wash me in Thy precious Blood,
   And take my sins away !

   A few more storms shall beat
   On this wild rocky shore,
And we shall be where tempests cease,
   And surges swell no more :

A few more Years shall roll.

Then, O my Lord, prepare
My soul for that calm day ;
Oh, wash me in Thy precious Blood,
And take my sins away !

A few more struggles here,
A few more partings o'er,
A few more toils, a few more tears,
And we shall weep no more :
Then, O my Lord, prepare
My soul for that bright day ;
Oh, wash me in Thy precious Blood,
And take my sins away !

'T is but a little while
And He shall come again,
Who died that we might live, Who lives
That we with Him may reign :
Then, O my Lord, prepare
My soul for that glad day ;
Oh, wash me in Thy precious Blood,
And take my sins away !

HORATIUS BONAR.

As pants the Hart for Cooling Streams.

S pants the hart for cooling streams,
 When heated in the chase,
So longs my soul, O God, for Thee
 And Thy refreshing grace.

For Thee, my God, the living God,
 My thirsty soul doth pine ;
Oh, when shall I behold Thy face,
 Thou Majesty divine?

Why restless, why cast down, my soul?
 Trust God, who will employ
His aid for Thee, and change these sighs
 To thankful hymns of joy.

God of my strength, how long shall I,
 Like one forgotten, mourn,
Forlorn, forsaken, and exposed
 To my oppressors' scorn?

As pants the Hart for Cooling Streams.

My heart is pierced as with a sword,
  While thus my foes upbraid :
" Vain boaster, where is now thy God?
  And where His promised aid?"

Why restless, why cast down, my soul?
  Hope still ; and thou shalt sing
The praise of Him who is Thy God,
  Thy health's eternal spring.

TATE AND BRADY. 1696.

125

O Mother dear, Jerusalem!

MOTHER dear, Jerusalem!
　　When shall I come to thee?
　When shall my sorrows have an end?
　　Thy joys when shall I see?

O happy harbor of God's saints!
　O sweet and pleasant soil!
In thee no sorrow can be found,
　Nor grief, nor care, nor toil.

No murky cloud o'ershadows thee.
　Nor gloom, nor darksome night;
But every soul shines as the sun,
　For God himself gives light.

O my sweet home, Jerusalem!
　Thy joys when shall I see?
The King that sitteth on thy throne
　In His felicity?

126

Thy gardens and thy goodly walks
  Continually are green,
Where grow such sweet and pleasant flowers
  As nowhere else are seen.

Right through the streets, with pleasing sound,
  The living waters flow,
And on the banks, on either side,
  The trees of life do grow.

Those trees each month yield ripened fruit,
  Forevermore they spring,
And all the nations of the earth
  To thee their honors bring.

O Mother dear, Jerusalem !
  When shall I come to thee?
When shall my sorrows have an end?
  Thy joys when shall I see?

Dawn purples all the East with Light.

DAWN purples all the east with light,
   Day o'er the earth is gliding bright,
   Morn's sparkling rays their course begin, —
Farewell to darkness and to sin !

Each evil dream of night, depart !
Each thought of guilt, forsake the heart !
Let every ill that darkness brought
Beneath its shade, now come to naught !

So that last morning, dread and great,
Which we with trembling hope await,
With blessèd light for us shall glow,
Who chant the song we learnt below.

O Father, that we ask be done,
Through Jesus Christ, Thine only Son,
Who, with the Holy Ghost and Thee,
Shall live and reign eternally !

St. Ambrose (Tr. Neale).

Virtue.

 WEET day, so cool, so calm, so bright,
The bridal of the earth and sky,
The dew shall weep thy fall to-night ;
For thou must die.

Sweet rose, whose hue, angry and brave,
Bids the rash gazer wipe his eye,
Thy root is ever in its grave, —
And thou must die.

Sweet spring, full of sweet days and roses,
A box where sweets compacted lie,
My music shows ye have your closes,
And all must die.

Only a sweet and virtuous soul,
Like seasoned timber, never gives ;
But, though the whole world turn to coal,
Then chiefly lives.

GEORGE HERBERT.

Hymn.

HRIST to the young man said : "Yet one
    thing more ;
  If thou wouldst perfect be,
Sell all thou hast and give it to the poor,
  And come and follow me !"

Within this temple Christ again, unseen,
  Those sacred words hath said,
And his invisible hands to-day have been
  Laid on a young man's head.

And evermore beside him on his way
  The unseen Christ shall move,
That he may lean upon his arm and say,
  "Dost Thou, dear Lord, approve?"

Beside him at the marriage feast shall be,
    To make the scene more fair ;
Beside him in the dark Gethsemane
    Of pain and midnight prayer.

O holy trust ! O endless sense of rest !
    Like the beloved John
To lay his head upon the Saviour's breast,
    And thus to journey on !

           H. W. LONGFELLOW.
              (For his brother's ordination).

A Sun-Day Hymn.

LORD of all being! throned afar,
   Thy glory flames from sun and star :
   Centre and soul of every sphere,
   Yet to each loving heart how near!

Sun of our life, thy quickening ray
Sheds on our path the glow of day ;
Star of our hope, thy softened light
Cheers the long watches of the night.

Our midnight is thy smile withdrawn :
Our noontide is thy gracious dawn :
Our rainbow arch thy mercy's sign ;
All, save the clouds of sin, are thine !

Lord of all life, below, above,
Whose light is truth, whose warmth is love,
Before thy ever-blazing throne
We ask no lustre of our own.

A Sun=Day Hymn.

Grant us thy truth to make us free,
And kindling hearts that burn for thee,
Till all thy living altars claim
One holy light, one heavenly flame!

OLIVER WENDELL HOLMES.

133

Hymn of Trust.

 LOVE Divine, that stooped to share
    Our sharpest pang, our bitterest tear,
On Thee we cast each earth-born care,
    We smile at pain while Thou art near!

Though long the weary way we tread,
    And sorrow crown each lingering year,
No path we shun, no darkness dread,
    Our hearts still whispering, Thou art near !

When drooping pleasure turns to grief,
    And trembling faith is changed to fear,
The murmuring wind, the quivering leaf,
    Shall softly tell us, Thou art near!

On Thee we fling our burdening woe,
    O Love Divine, forever dear,
Content to suffer while we know,
    Living and dying, Thou art near!

OLIVER WENDELL HOLMES.

The Crucifixion.

SUNLIGHT upon Judæa's hills,
   And on the waves of Galilee !
On Jordan's stream, and on the rills
   That feed the dead and sleeping sea !
Most freshly from the greenwood springs
The light breeze on its scented wings ;
And gayly quiver in the sun
The cedar tops of Lebanon !

A few more hours, — a change hath come !
   The sky is dark without a cloud !
The shouts of wrath and joy are dumb,
   And proud knees unto earth are bowed.
A change is on the hill of Death,
The helméd watchers pant for breath,
And turn with wild and maniac eyes
From the dark scene of sacrifice !

That Sacrifice ! — the death of Him, —
   The Christ of God, the Holy One !
Well may the conscious Heaven grow dim,
   And blacken the beholding Sun.

The Crucifixion.

The wonted light hath fled away,
Night settles on the middle day,
And Earthquake from his caverned bed
Is waking with a thrill of dread!

The dead are waking underneath!
  Their prison door is rent away!
And, ghastly with the seal of death,
  They wander in the eye of day!
The temple of the Cherubim,
The House of God is cold and dim:
A curse is on its trembling walls,
Its mighty veil asunder falls!

Well may the cavern depths of earth
  Be shaken, and her mountains nod:
Well may the sheeted dead come forth
  To see the suffering Son of God!
Well may the temple shrine grow dim,
And shadows veil the Cherubim,
When He, the chosen One of Heaven,
A sacrifice for guilt is given!

And shall the sinful heart, alone,
  Behold unmoved the fearful hour,
When Nature trembled on her throne,
  And Death resigned his iron power?

Oh, shall the heart — whose sinfulness
Gave keenness to His sore distress,
And added to His tears of blood —
Refuse its trembling gratitude !

JOHN GREENLEAF WHITTIER.

137

From Every Stormy Wind that Blows.

ROM every stormy wind that blows,
From every swelling tide of woes,
There is a calm, a sure retreat ;
'T is found beneath the mercy-seat.

There is a place where Jesus sheds
The oil of gladness on our heads, —
A place than all beside more sweet,
It is the bloodstained mercy-seat.

There is a spot where spirits blend,
Where friend holds fellowship with friend ;
Though sundered far, by faith they meet
Around one common mercy-seat.

There, there, on eagles' wings we soar,
And time and sense seem all no more ;
And heaven comes down, our souls to greet,
And glory crowns the mercy-seat.

HUGH STOWELL.

138

The Son of God goes forth to War.

THE Son of God goes forth to war,
  A kingly crown to gain :
His blood-red banner streams afar,
  Who follows in His train !
Who best can drink his cup of woe,
  Triumphant over pain,
Who patient bears his cross below,
  He follows in His train.

The martyr first, whose eagle eye
  Could pierce beyond the grave,
Who saw his Master in the sky,
  And called on Him to save :
Like Him, with pardon on his tongue,
  In midst of mortal pain,
He prayed for them that did the wrong :
  Who follows in his train?

139

The Son of God goes forth to War.

A glorious band, the chosen few,
  On whom the Spirit came :
Twelve valiant saints, their hope they knew,
  And mocked the cross and flame :
They met the tyrant's brandished steel,
  The lion's gory mane :
They bowed their necks the death to feel :
  Who follows in their train?

A noble army, men and boys,
  The matron and the maid,
Around the Saviour's throne rejoice,
  In robes of light arrayed :
They climbed the steep ascent of heaven
  Through peril, toil, and pain :
O God ! to us may grace be given
  To follow in their train !

REGINALD HEBER.

Oh, Worship the King.

H, worship the King,
      All glorious above !
  Oh, gratefully sing
      His power and His love.
Our Shield and Defender,
  The Ancient of days,
Pavilioned in splendor,
  And girded with praise.

Oh, tell of His might,
  Oh, sing of His grace,
Whose robe is the light,
  Whose canopy space !
His chariots of wrath
  Deep thunder-clouds form
And dark is His path
  On the wings of the storm.

The earth, with its store
  Of wonders untold,
Almighty, Thy power
  Hath founded of old, —

Oh, Worship the King.

Hath stablished it fast
    By a changeless decree,
And round it hath cast.
    Like a mantle, the sea.

Thy bountiful care
    What tongue can recite?
It breathes in the air,
    It shines in the light ;
It streams from the hills.
    It descends to the plain.
And sweetly distils
    In the dew and the rain.

Frail children of dust,
    And feeble as frail,
In Thee do we trust,
    Nor find Thee to fail ;
Thy mercies, how tender,
    How firm to the end.
Our Maker, Defender,
    Redeemer, and Friend !

O measureless might.
    Ineffable Love !
While angels delight
    To hymn Thee above,

The ransomed creation,
  Though feeble their lays,
With true adoration
  Shall lisp to Thy praise.

SIR ROBERT GRANT.

143

Psalm 121.

P to those bright and gladsome hills,
 Whence flows my weal and mirth,
I look and sigh for Him, who fills
 Unseen both heaven and earth.

He is alone my help and hope,
 That I shall not be moved ;
His watchful eye is ever ope,
 And guardeth his beloved.

The glorious God is my sole stay,
 He is my sun and shade ;
The cold by night, the heat by day,
 Neither shall me invade.

He keeps me from the spite of foes,
 Doth all their plots control ;
And is a shield, not reckoning those,
 Unto my very soul.

144

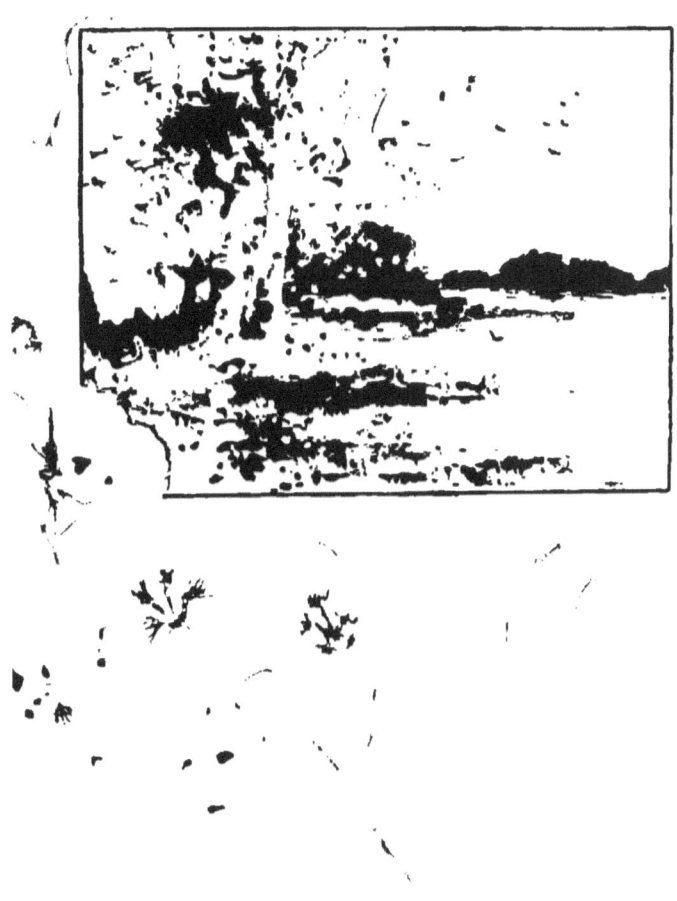

Whether abroad, amidst the crowd,
  Or else within my door,
He is my pillar and my cloud,
  Now and forevermore.

HENRY VAUGHAN.

A Mighty Fortress is our God.

MIGHTY fortress is our God,
A bulwark never failing;
Our helper He amid the flood
Of mortal ills prevailing.
For still our ancient foe
Doth seek to work us woe;
His craft and power are great;
And, armed with cruel hate,
On earth is not his equal.

Did we in our own strength confide,
Our striving would be losing;
Were not the right man on our side, —
The man of God's own choosing.
Dost ask who that may be?
Christ Jesus: it is he;
Lord Sabaoth his name,
From age to age the same,
And he must win the battle.

And though this world, with devils filled,
   Should threaten to undo us,
We will not fear ; for God hath willed
   His truth to triumph through us,
The Prince of Darkness grim, —
We tremble not for him :
His rage we can endure,
For, lo ! his doom is sure :
   One little word shall fell him.

That word above all earthly powers —
   No thanks to them — abideth ;
The spirit and the gifts are ours,
   Through Him who with us sideth.
Let goods and kindred go,
This mortal life also :
The body they may kill,
God's truth abideth still ;
   His kingdom is forever.

MARTIN LUTHER.
(Tr. F. H. HEDGE.)

When Israel, of the Lord beloved.

HEN Israel, of the Lord beloved.
　　Out of the land of bondage came,
Her fathers' God before her moved.
　　An awful guide, in smoke and flame.
By day, along the astonished lands
　　The cloudy pillar glided slow ;
By night, Arabia's crimsoned sands
　　Returned the fiery column's glow.

There rose the choral hymn of praise,
　　And trump and timbrel answered keen,
And Zion's daughters poured their lays.
　　With priest's and warrior's voice between.
No portents now our foes amaze.
　　Forsaken Israel wanders lone ;
Our fathers would not know Thy ways,
　　And Thou hast left them to their own.

But present still, though now unseen,
　　When brightly shines the prosperous day,
Be thoughts of Thee a cloudy screen
　　To temper the deceitful ray.
And oh, when stoops on Judah's path
　　In shade and storm the frequent night,
Be Thou, long-suffering, slow to wrath,
　　A burning and a shining light!

Our harps we left by Babel's streams,
　　The tyrant's jest, the Gentile's scorn ;
No censer round our altar beams,
　　And mute our timbrel, trump, and horn.
But Thou hast said, the blood of goat,
　　The flesh of rams, I will not prize ;
A contrite heart, an humble thought,
　　Are mine accepted sacrifice.

SIR WALTER SCOTT.

The King of Love my Shepherd is.

HE King of love my Shepherd is,
   Whose goodness faileth never ;
I nothing lack if I am His,
   And He is mine forever.

Where streams of living water flow
   My ransomed soul He leadeth.
And, where the verdant pastures grow,
   With food celestial feedeth.

Perverse and foolish, oft I strayed,
   But yet in love He sought me.
And on His shoulder gently laid,
   And home, rejoicing, brought me.

In death's dark vale I fear no ill
   With Thee, dear Lord, beside me ;
Thy rod and staff my comfort still,
   Thy Cross before to guide me.

Thou spread'st a table in my sight,
  Thy unction grace bestoweth,
And oh the transport of delight
  With which my cup o'erfloweth!

And so, through all the length of days,
  Thy goodness faileth never;
Good Shepherd, may I sing Thy praise
  Within Thy house forever!

Sir H. W. Baker

Take up thy Cross.

THOU say'st, "Take up thy cross,
　　O man, and follow Me;"
The night is black, the feet are slack,
　　Yet we would follow Thee.

But, O dear Lord, we cry,
　　That we Thy face could see!
Thy blessèd face one moment's space, —
　　Then might we follow Thee!

Dim tracts of time divide
　　Those golden days from me;
Thy voice comes strange o'er years of change;
　　How can we follow Thee?

Comes faint and far Thy voice
　　From vales of Galilee;
Thy vision fades in ancient shades;
　　How should we follow Thee?

O heavy cross — of faith
  In what we cannot see !
As once of yore Thyself restore
  And help to follow Thee !

If not as once Thou cam'st
  In true humanity,
Come yet as guest within the breast
  That burns to follow Thee.

Within our heart of hearts
  In nearest nearness be ;
Set up Thy throne within Thine own ;
  Go, Lord ; we follow Thee.   Amen.

F. T. PALGRAVE.

Beyond that boundless Sea.

BEYOND, beyond that boundless sea,
    Above that dome of sky,
  Farther than thought itself can flee,
    Thy dwelling is on high :
Yet dear the awful thought to me,
    That Thou, my God, art nigh ; —

Art nigh, and yet my laboring mind
    Feels after Thee in vain,
Thee in these works of power to find,
    Or to Thy seat attain.
Thy messenger, the stormy wind ;
    Thy path, the trackless main :

These speak of Thee with loud acclaim ;
    They thunder forth Thy praise,
The glorious honor of Thy name,
    The wonders of Thy ways :
But Thou art not in tempest flame,
    Nor in the noontide blaze.

We hear Thy voice when thunders roll
Through the wide fields of air;
The waves obey Thy dread control;
But still, Thou art not there:
Where shall I find Him, O my soul!
Who yet is everywhere?

Oh! not in circling depth or height,
But in the conscious breast,
Present to faith, though veiled from sight,
There doth His Spirit rest:
Oh, come, thou Presence infinite!
And make Thy creature blest.

EUSTACE CONDER.

155

Father, I know that all my life.

FATHER, I know that all my life
    Is portioned out for me;
The changes that will surely come,
    I do not fear to see:
I ask Thee for a present mind,
    Intent on pleasing Thee.

I ask Thee for a thoughtful love,
    Through constant watching wise,
To meet the glad with joyful smiles,
    And wipe the weeping eyes;
A heart at leisure from itself,
    To soothe and sympathize.

I would not have the restless will
    That hurries to and fro,
That seeks for some great thing to do,
    Or secret thing to know;
I would be treated as a child,
    And guided where I go.

Father, I know that all my life.

Wherever in the world I am,
    In whatsoe'er estate,
I have a fellowship with hearts
    To keep and cultivate,
A work of lowly love to do
    For Him on whom I wait.

I ask Thee for the daily strength,
    To none that ask denied,
A mind to blend with outward life,
    While keeping at Thy side;
Content to fill a little space,
    If Thou be glorified.

And if some things I do not ask
    Among my blessings be,
I 'd have my spirit filled the more
    With grateful love to Thee;
More careful, not to serve Thee much,
    But please Thee perfectly.

A. L. WARING.

City of God, how broad and far.

ITY of God, how broad and far
Outspread Thy walls sublime !
The true Thy chartered freemen are,
Of every age and clime.

One holy Church, one army strong,
One steadfast high intent,
One working band, one harvest song,
One King Omnipotent !

How purely hath Thy speech come down
From man's primeval youth !
How grandly hath Thine empire grown,
Of Freedom, Love, and Truth !

How gleam Thy watch-fires through the night
With never-fainting ray !
How rise Thy towers, serene and bright,
To meet the dawning day !

In vain the surges' angry shock,
  In vain the drifting sands;
Unharmed upon the Eternal Rock
  The Eternal City stands. Amen.

SAMUEL JOHNSON.

Dies Iræ.

AY of Wrath, — that Day of Days, —
When earth shall vanish in a blaze,
As David, with the Sibyl, says!

What a trembling will come o'er us,
When the Judge shall be before us,
For every hidden sin to score us!

The trumpet with its wondrous sound,
Piercing each sepulchral mound,
Shall summon all, the throne around.

Nature and death will stand aghast,
When those who to the grave have past,
Come answering to the judgment blast!

The written Book shall be unrolled,
Wherein the deeds of all are told,
And shall the doom of all unfold.

For when the Judge shall be enthroned,
No secret shall be left unowned,
No crime or trespass unatoned.

Then for a guilty wretch like me,
What plea, what pleader, will there be,
When scarcely shall the just go free!

King of tremendous majesty,
Whose grace saves all who saved may be,
Fountain of mercy, oh save me!

Forget not then, dear Son of God,
For my sake Thou thy way hast trod,
Nor let me sink beneath thy rod.

Yes, me to save Thou sat'st in pain,
Nor didst the bitter Cross disdain, —
Let not such anguish be in vain!

Unerring Judge, thy wrath restrain,
And let my sins remission gain,
While still the days of grace remain.

Dies Iræ.

I groan as one condemned to die,
In vain to hide my shame I try,
Lord, listen to my suppliant cry!

Thou who the Magdalen forgave,
And joy'd the dying thief to save,
Hast given me hope beyond the grave.

All my prayers are empty shows,
But let thy mercy interpose,
And spare me from eternal woes.

Among the sheep, oh let me stand,
Far from the goats' accursed band, —
And taste the joys of thy right hand!

While the guilty are appalled,
And to endless flames inthralled,
Oh let me with the blest be called!

Prostrate at thy feet I lie,
My contrite heart as ashes dry,
Care for me when the end draws nigh!

That, that will be a day of gloom,
When man, to meet his final doom,
Shall rise, all-guilty, from the grave, —
Spare him, God, oh spare and save !

Tr. Robert C. Winthrop.

163

Evening.

EHOLD the sun, that seemed but now
  Enthronèd overhead,
    Beginneth to decline below
  The globe whereon we tread ;
And he, whom yet we look upon
  With comfort and delight,
Will quite depart from hence anon,
  And leave us to the night.

Thus time, unheeded, steals away
  The life which Nature gave ;
Thus are our bodies every day
  Declining to the grave ; .
Thus from us all our pleasures fly
  Whereon we set our heart,
And when the night of death draws nigh,
  Thus will they all depart.

Lord ! though the sun forsake our sight,
  And mortal hopes are vain,
Let still Thine everlasting light
  Within our souls remain !
And in the nights of our distress
  Vouchsafe those rays divine
Which from the Sun of Righteousness
  Forever brightly shine.

G. WITHER.

Crossing the Bar.

SUNSET and evening star,
And one clear call for me !
And may there be no moaning of the bar
When I put out to sea,

But such a tide as moving seems asleep,
Too full for sound and foam,
When that which drew from out the boundless deep
Turns again home.

Twilight and evening bell,
And after that the dark !
And may there be no sadness or farewell,
When I embark ;

For though from out our bourne of Time and Place
The flood may bear me far,
I hope to see my Pilot face to face
When I have crost the bar.

LORD TENNYSON.
(Sung at his funeral.)

Upon the Hills the Wind is Sharp and Cold.

PON the hills the wind is sharp and cold,
The sweet young grasses wither on the
wold.
And we, O Lord, have wandered from
Thy fold ;
But evening brings us home.

We have been wounded by the hunter's darts ;
Our eyes are heavy, and our longing hearts
Search for Thy coming !   When the light departs
At evening, bring us home.

The darkness gathers ; through the gloom no star
Shines on our path, and we have wandered far ;
Without Thy lamp we know not where we are,
But evening brings us home.

Upon the Hills the Wind is Sharp and Cold.

The clouds are round us, and the snowdrifts thicken;
O Thou dear Shepherd, leave us not to sicken;
Waste is the night, — Thy saving footsteps quicken;
    At evening bring us home.

AUTHOR UNKNOWN.

168

O God, our Help in Ages past.

GOD, our help in ages past,
  Our hope for years to come,
Our shelter from the stormy blast,
  And our eternal home :

Under the shadow of Thy throne
  Thy saints have dwelt secure ;
Sufficient is Thine arm alone,
  And our defence is sure.

Before the hills in order stood,
  Or earth received her frame,
From everlasting Thou art God,
  To endless years the same.

A thousand ages in Thy sight
  Are like an evening gone,
Short as the watch that ends the night
  Before the rising sun.

O God, our Help in Ages past.

Time, like an ever rolling stream,
　Bears all its sons away;
They fly forgotten, as a dream
　Dies at the opening day.

O God, our help in ages past,
　Our hope for years to come,
Be Thou our Guard while life shall last,
　And our eternal home!

ISAAC WATTS.
(Sung at the funeral of BISHOP BROOKS.)

Come Quickly, Sweetest Lord.

EVER weather-beaten sail more willing bent to
    shore,
    Never tired pilgrim's limbs affected slumber
    more,
Than my wearied sprite now longs to fly out of my
    troubled breast.
Oh, come quickly, sweetest Lord, and take my soul to
    rest!

Ever blooming are the joys of heaven's high Paradise;
Cold age deafs not there our ears, nor vapor dims our
    eyes;
Glory there the sun outshines; whose beams the Blessed
    only see.
Oh, come quickly, glorious Lord, and raise my sprite
    to Thee!

THOMAS CAMPION.

Do I not love Thee, Lord Most High?

O I not love Thee, Lord most High,
In answer to Thy love for me?
I seek no other liberty
But that of being bound to Thee.

May memory no thought suggest
   But shall to Thy pure glory tend;
My understanding find no rest
   Except in Thee, its only end.

My God, I here protest to Thee,
   No other will I have than Thine;
Whatever Thou hast given me
   I here again to Thee resign.

All mine is Thine; say but the word;
   Whate'er Thou willest, — be it done.
I know Thy love, all-gracious Lord, —
   I know it seeks my good alone.

Apart from Thee all things are nought;
Then grant, O my supremest bliss!
Grant me to love Thee as I ought : —
Thou givest all in giving this!

IGNATIUS LOYOLA.
(Translated by E. CASWALL.)

173

Maker of the Human Heart.

AKER of the human heart,
    Scorn not Thou Thine own creation;
Onward guide its nobler part,
    Train it for its high vocation:
From the long infected grain
Cleanse and purge each sinful stain
Kindle with a kindred fire
Every good and great desire!

When in ruin and in gloom
    Falls to dust our earthly mansion,
Give us ample verge and room
    For the measureless expansion;
Clear our clouded mental sight
To endure Thy piercing light;
Open wide our narrow thought
To embrace Thee as we ought!

174

Maker of the Human Heart.

When the shadows melt away,
   And the Eternal Day is breaking,
Judge, most Just, be Thou our stay
   In that strange and solemn waking!
Thou to whom the heart sincere
Is Thy best of temples here,
May Thy faithfulness and love
Be our long last home above!

ARTHUR PENRHYN STANLEY.

Out of the Depths I cry to Thee.

OUT of the depths I cry to Thee;
Lord, hear me, I implore Thee!
Bend down Thy gracious ear to me, —
Let my prayer come before Thee!
If Thou rememb'rest each misdeed,
If each should have its rightful meed,
Who may abide Thy presence?

Our pardon is Thy gift; Thy love
And grace alone avail us;
Our works could ne'er our guilt remove,
The strictest life must fail us:
That none may boast himself of aught,
But own in fear Thy grace hath wrought
What in him seemeth righteous.

And thus my hope is in the Lord.
And not in mine own merit;
I rest upon His faithful word
To them of contrite spirit.

That He is merciful and just,
Here is my comfort and my trust ;
   His help I wait with patience.

Though great our sins and sore our woes,
   His grace much more aboundeth ;
His helping love no limit knows,
   Our utmost need it soundeth ;
Our kind and faithful Shepherd, He
Who shall at last set Israel free
   From all their sin and sorrow.

MARTIN LUTHER.
(Translated by C. WINKWORTH.)

www.ingramcontent.com/pod-product-compliance
Lightning Source LLC
Chambersburg PA
CBHW030634030726
47497CB00006B/1781